This book is a work of fiction. Any references to historical events, real people, or real places are used fictitiously. Other names, characters, places, and events are products of the author's imagination, and any resemblance to actual events or places or persons, living or dead, is entirely coincidental.

LITTLE SIMON

An imprint of Simon & Schuster Children's Publishing Division • 1230 Avenue of the Americas, New York, New York 10020 • First Little Simon paperback edition June 2024 • Copyright © 2024 by Simon & Schuster, LLC • All rights reserved, including the right of reproduction in whole or in part in any form. LITTLE SIMON is a registered trademark of Simon & Schuster, Inc., and associated colophon is a trademark of Simon & Schuster, LLC. • Simon & Schuster: Celebrating 100 Years of Publishing in 2024 • For information about special discounts for bulk purchases, please contact Simon & Schuster Special Sales at 1-866-506-1949 or business@simonandschuster.com. The Simon & Schuster Speakers Bureau can bring authors to your live event. For more information or to book an event contact the Simon & Schuster Speakers Bureau at 1-866-248-3049 or visit our website at www.simonspeakers.com.
Series designed by Laura Roode.
Book designed by Chani Yammer. The text of this book was set in Usherwood.
Manufactured in the United States of America 0524 LAK
10 9 8 7 6 5 4 3 2 1
Names: Green, Poppy, author. | Bell, Jennifer A., illustrator.
Title: Lightning Bug light show / by Poppy Green ; illustrated by Jennifer A. Bell.
Description: First Little Simon paperback edition. | New York : Little Simon, 2024. | Series: The adventures of Sophie Mouse ; book 21 | Audience: Ages 5-9. | Audience: Grades K-1. | Summary: Sophie Mouse helps a self-conscious firefly discover the beauty of his bright glow just in time for him to perform with his Lightning Bug troupe.
Identifiers: LCCN 2023036341 (print) | LCCN 2023036342 (ebook) | ISBN 9781665953054 (paperback) | ISBN 9781665953061 (hardcover) | ISBN 9781665953078 (ebook)
Subjects: CYAC: Mice—Fiction. | Fireflies—Fiction. | Animals—Fiction. | Theater—Fiction. | Self-consciousness—Fiction. | LCGFT: Animal fiction.
Classification: LCC PZ7.G82616 Li 2024 (print) | LCC PZ7.G82616 (ebook) | DDC [Fic]—dc23 LC record available at https://lccn.loc.gov/2023036341 LC ebook record available at https://lccn.loc.gov/202303634

the adventures of
SOPHIE MOUSE

21

Lightning Bug Light Show

By Poppy Green • Illustrated by Jennifer A. Bell

LITTLE SIMON

New York London Toronto Sydney New Delhi

Contents

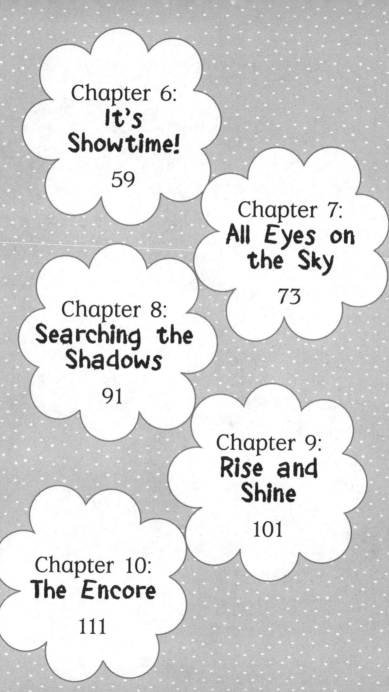

— Chapter 1 —

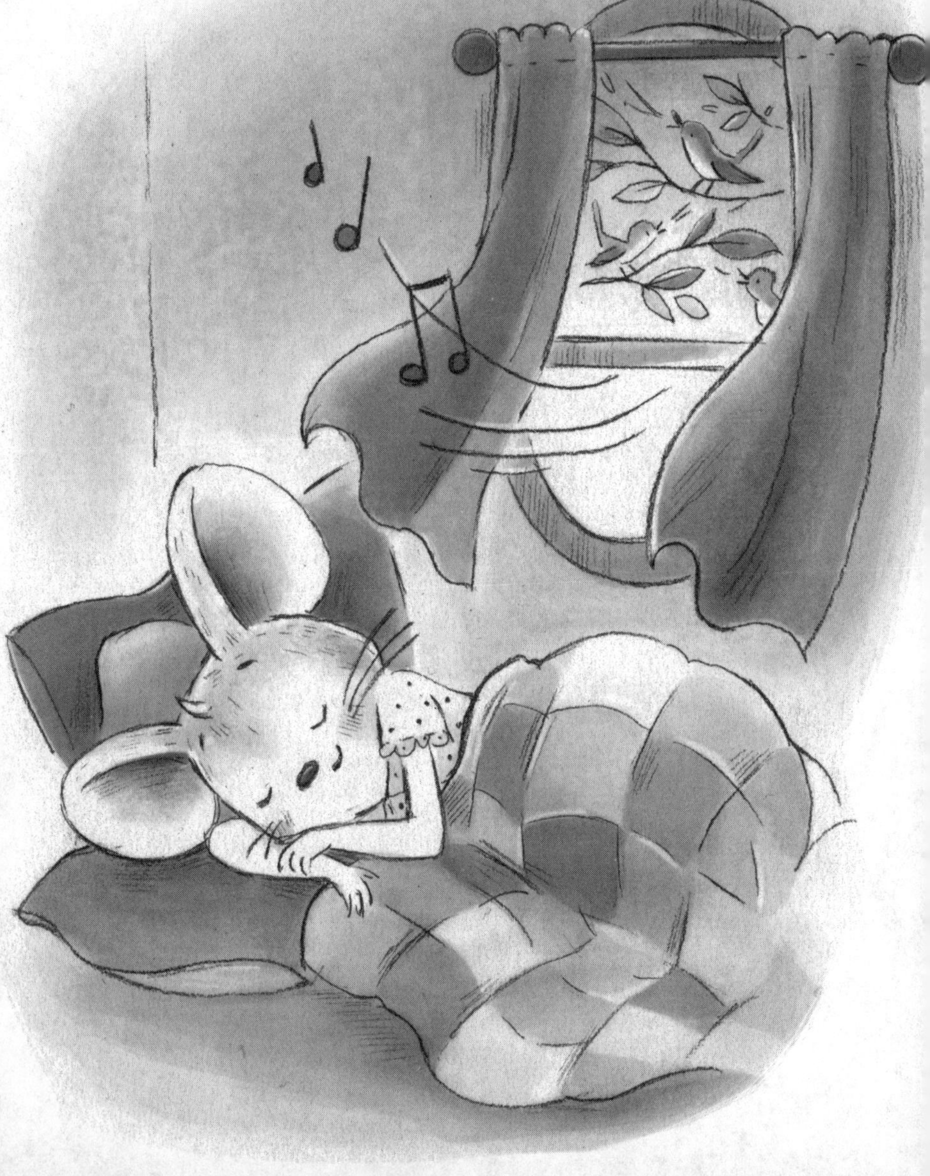

New Show in Town

Sophie Mouse rolled over in bed. Her dandelion-puff blanket had shifted overnight from a breeze that swept through the open window. The sweet scent of dewy trees wafted in.

The birds chirped their morning songs and then came new sounds: a cracking of twigs and rustling of leaves.

The sounds kept growing louder
and louder. Sophie pulled her blanket
over her head.

What was making those sounds?

Whatever it was, now it sounded close, like it was right outside Sophie's window in the big old oak tree.

Sophie sat up and rubbed her eyes. She pulled her window curtains apart and looked out.

Rolling past her house was a big yellow wagon. Right behind it was another. And another!

Sophie blinked three times. She had never seen such big wagons before. Could she be dreaming?

Sophie climbed down from her bed. Still just half awake, she felt around in her closet. She grabbed her robe and put it on. Then she stumbled down the stairs and through the kitchen. She threw open the front door.

The forest was peaceful and still.

Sophie ran down the front path. She peered down the forest trail. The wagons were just . . . gone!

"Good morning, Sophie." Sophie's dad appeared at the front door. Her little brother, Winston, followed close behind.

"Dad!" Sophie exclaimed. "I saw wagons rolling past our house!"

Winston ran outside to join her. "Where?" he cried.

Sophie shook her head. "They're gone now," she replied. "But I saw them. Honest!"

"Wagons, you say?" said George Mouse. His eyes twinkled, and his whiskers twitched.

Sophie and Winston followed their dad back inside the house. "Dad, what is it?" Sophie said. "What do you know?"

George Mouse sat down at the table. "Those wagons mean the Lightning Bugs have arrived!"

Sophie's ears perked up. "Lightning Bugs?" she said. "Like, fireflies?"

"A very special troupe of fireflies,"
Mr. Mouse explained. "They go from
town to town as traveling performers.
They put on an amazing light show!
Here, I'll show you."

He pulled out
a scrapbook from
the bookshelf
and flipped
through it.
He stopped
on a page
with a ticket
stub pasted
on it.

"This is from the very first Lightning Bug show I saw," Mr. Mouse told them. "I was about your age, Sophie." Then he laughed. "I wore a headlamp for weeks afterward, because I wanted to glow just like a lightning bug."

Sophie studied the ticket stub. A light show at night! It sounded magical.

"Well," Winston said, "if the Lightning Bugs are here, that means they'll be performing here. Right, Dad?"

Sophie gasped. "Oh, can we go, Dad?" she pleaded. "Please?"

— Chapter 2 —

Sneaky Snakes and Other Surprises

Mr. Mouse thought it over. "The Lightning Bugs perform after dark, so the show starts quite late." He paused. "I think you're old enough to go this year, Sophie. But Winston, I think it's best if you stay home with Mom."

Sophie clapped and jumped for joy. But Winston pouted and crossed his arms.

"How about this, Winston?" Sophie said. "At the show, I'll pay attention to every detail. Then I'll make a painting of the light show for you."

Winston didn't uncross his arms. But his pout disappeared, and he nodded. Winston loved Sophie's paintings.

After breakfast, Sophie hurried to find her friends at the stream. Hattie Frog was already there, of course. Her family's house sat right on the bank of the stream.

Hattie was braiding reeds when Sophie sat down next to her. Just then, the trees above them rustled. Sophie and Hattie looked up in alarm.

"What's going on up there?" Sophie wondered aloud.

Suddenly, a friendly face popped out from the dense leaves. It was Owen Snake!

"Did you know it was me?" he asked, grinning widely.

Hattie breathed a sigh of relief. "Don't scare me like that!" she scolded Owen.

He slithered down the tree trunk and said, "Come on. It's fun! It's a new game I call sneaky snake. I hide in a sneaky spot. I win if no one can find me, or if I can surprise them before they find me."

Now that her friends were both here, Sophie told Hattie and Owen all about the Lightning Bug wagons.

"They're putting on a show in Silverlake Forest," Sophie said. "Dad said he would take me!"

Hattie and Owen promised to ask their parents if they could attend too.

"But when is it?" Hattie asked.

"Let's go find out," Owen suggested.

Sophie had an idea. She led the way back to her house and pointed to wagon wheel tracks on the ground. "We'll follow these," said Sophie. "They'll lead us to the Lightning Bugs."

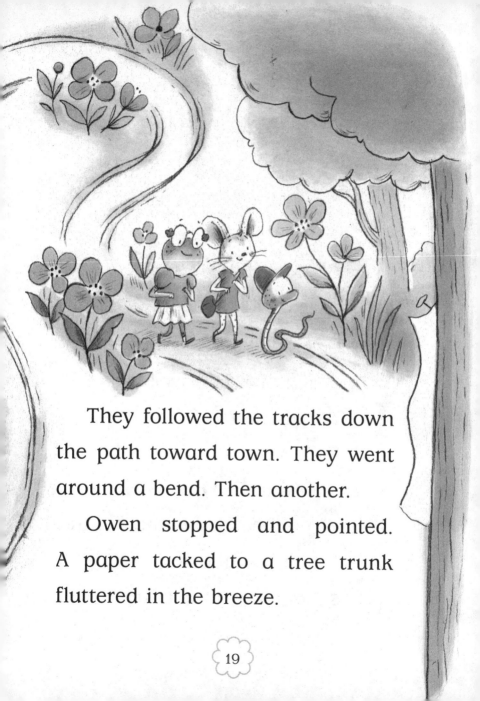

They followed the tracks down the path toward town. They went around a bend. Then another.

Owen stopped and pointed. A paper tacked to a tree trunk fluttered in the breeze.

COME SEE THE LIGHT SHOW BY THE

LIGHTNING BUGS!

WHERE: GOLDMOSS POND

WHEN: FRIDAY, AFTER DARK

ONE DAY ONLY!

Close to town, they came around
another bend. Up ahead, a lightning
bug was hanging up another flyer.

He looked only a few years older than Sophie.

"Hello there!" Sophie called out.

The lightning bug jumped up in alarm. He dropped his armload of flyers. They fell into muddy leaves.

Frantically, the lightning bug reached down to pick them up. But he lost his balance and stepped on the flyers instead.

"Oh no!" cried the lightning bug. "Oh no, oh no!"

— Chapter 3 —

Welcome to Silverlake Forest

Sophie, Hattie, and Owen rushed to the lightning bug's side.

"Sorry we startled you!" Hattie said. She started picking up the muddy flyers.

The bug fanned one of the papers, trying to dry it. "It's all my fault," he said, flustered. "I get startled easily."

"I'm Sophie, and this is Hattie and Owen. Are you part of the Lightning Bugs?" Sophie asked him.

He nodded. "I'm Rory," he said. Then he pointed at the muddy flyers. "I was supposed to hang all of these.

LIGHTNING BUG LIGHT SHOW!

But now they're ruined and no one will know about our show."

Sophie beamed. "Well, I'll be at the show!" she exclaimed. "So will my dad. And maybe Hattie and Owen."

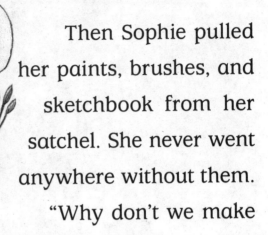

Then Sophie pulled her paints, brushes, and sketchbook from her satchel. She never went anywhere without them.

"Why don't we make new flyers?" Sophie suggested.

Rory's eyes went wide. "Really? You would do that for me?"

Hattie and Owen eagerly nodded.

They spread the paper, paint, and brushes out on a patch of grass nearby. Then they all got to work. Before long, they had created a stack of colorful new flyers.

"They look even more beautiful than the first flyers," Rory said. "Thank you!"

Sophie and her friends decided to help Rory hang up the new flyers. As they went, they gave him a tour of Silverlake Forest.

They passed near Hattie's house. "My parents designed it with Sophie's dad," Hattie explained. "Mr. Mouse is an architect."

Rory was impressed.

"Once, we performed in a village where everyone lived in mushroom houses," Rory told them. "It was hard to tell them apart."

Sophie tried to imagine that. What if all the homes in Silverlake Forest looked the same? Her dad's job would be simpler, but not as interesting!

They hung up more flyers near Forget-Me-Not Lake. "This is the biggest body of water in Silverlake Forest," Owen pointed out.

"I think the biggest body of water I've seen is the ocean," Rory said.

Sophie stopped in her tracks.

"You've been to the ocean?" she asked. "Does it really go on and on as far as you can see? Does the water really taste like salt? Were there waves? What *is* a wave, anyway?"

Rory took a half-step back with each question.

"Sorry," said Sophie sheepishly. "I've just never seen the ocean before!"

Eventually, they found themselves near Crystal Cave. Hattie wanted to show Rory the glowing crystals inside the dark cave.

"We don't have a lantern," Hattie said to Rory. "But you can light the way, can't you?"

Rory hesitated. "Actually, I should head back to the wagons," he said. "My dad will start looking for me soon."

He thanked them for all their help and for the tour of the forest.

"I've seen lots of places on the road," Rory said. "But I think Silverlake Forest is one of the prettiest!"

~ Chapter 4 ~

Sleepy Snake

The next morning, Sophie sat at her desk inside Silverlake Elementary. It was one of the last school days before summer vacation.

Mrs. Wise was taking attendance.

"Sophie Mouse?" she called out.

Sophie was gazing out the open window near her desk.

"Sophie?" Mrs. Wise said again.

Hattie leaned over and nudged
Sophie.

"What? Oh!" Sophie sat up in her
chair. "Here!"

Sophie was "here," but not "here."
In her mind, she was in a yellow
wagon, rolling down a woodsy path.
Up ahead, the woods opened up onto
a beach. A beach on the ocean!

She kept thinking about Rory's traveling life. She imagined how thrilling it would be to see so many places. She would never run out of new things to paint!

After Mrs. Wise had checked off Winston, Willy Toad, and Ellie Squirrel, Sophie finally noticed that Owen's seat was still empty.

Sophie looked at Hattie and frowned. Owen was never late to school.

Just then, the schoolhouse door flew open wide.

"Sorry, Mrs. Wise!" Owen called out breathlessly. He wriggled over to his desk and slid sheepishly into his seat.

Luckily, Mrs. Wise let Owen off with just a stern look over her glasses. But Sophie and Hattie were more curious.

At recess, they followed Owen outside. "Why were you tardy?" Hattie asked him.

"Never mind that," Owen replied. "Want to play sneaky snake?"

Before they could answer, Owen slid away. So Hattie and Sophie closed their eyes and counted to twenty.

"Ready or not, here we come!" Sophie called out. They looked behind the benches near the playground. Owen wasn't there.

They searched around the seesaw. They checked inside the play tunnel and under the picnic tables. No Owen.

"He is so good at this game," Sophie said. They took a rest on the schoolhouse steps.

"Oh!" said Hattie. "I asked my parents about the light show. They said we can go!"

Sophie clapped her hands in excitement. Suddenly, Owen popped out from behind the schoolhouse door. Hattie and Sophie jumped.

"Aaah!" Hattie cried.

Sophie laughed. "Okay, Owen. You win."

But Owen didn't look so happy. He had overheard what Hattie said.

Owen coiled up next to Sophie. "I asked my mom about the light show too," he said. "She said it's too late at night. So last night I stayed up way past my bedtime. To prove I *could* stay up late!"

Sophie put an arm around him. "But your mom didn't change her mind?"

Owen shook his head. "No. Especially because I had trouble waking up this morning."

So *that's* why Owen had been late to school. "I'm sorry you can't join us," Hattie said.

Sophie nodded. "Me too," she said. Then she told Owen about the painting she promised Winston. "I can make one for you, too."

Owen thought it over.

Then he yawned a tremendous yawn. It was so huge that Hattie and Sophie had to laugh. Even Owen laughed at himself.

"With jaws that unhinge, snakes are experts at yawning!" Owen said.

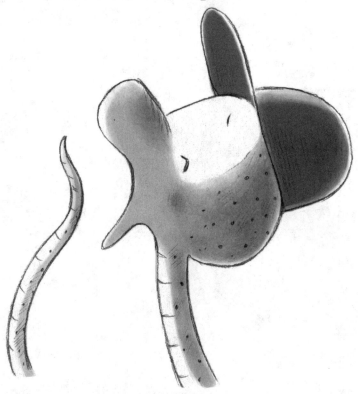

— Chapter 5 —

Rory's Life on Wheels

After school, Owen came up with a great idea. His house wasn't far from Goldmoss Pond, where the light show would be.

"That must be where the wagons are parked too," Owen said. "Since I can't go to the show, maybe I'll go see Rory on my way home instead."

Sophie and Hattie tagged along.

They took a route through town. That way, they could stop at Mrs. Mouse's bakery. She gladly handed them each a muffin of the day.

"Mmmm, lavender berry muffins!" said Sophie.

Then Sophie and her friends walked on. Through the buttercup patch, past the orchard, and on to Goldmoss Pond.

"There they are!" Owen cried out.
All the yellow wagons were parked
around the pond. "There must be
ten! Or more!"

As they got closer, they could see
all the lightning bugs. They looked

busy, zipping here and there. Some were doing jumping jacks. Some were stretching. Others were setting up ticket tables and food stands.

"This is going to be quite the show," Hattie said.

"And I'm going to miss it," Owen groaned.

"Oooh, there's Rory!" Sophie exclaimed. He was coming out of one of the wagons.

Sophie waved, and Rory hurried over to greet them. "We just got out of school," she told him.

"Me too!" Rory replied. "Sort of. I'm homeschooled. I just finished my lessons for today. Want to see our wagon?"

Inside the wagon, everything was set up so it was a home *and* a school on wheels. The fold-down table was also a desk. Book bins were hidden under the bed mattress. A cupboard door was painted so it could also be used as a chalkboard.

"There's a perfect place for everything," Hattie remarked.

Owen was more interested in seeing where the show would take place. "My mom won't let me come," he complained. "Do you think you could give me a sneak peek of your part in the show?"

Sophie clapped. "Oh yes!" she said. "I would love that too!"

But Rory looked down at his feet. "I can't," he said sadly. "Because I'm not performing."

Rory started to glow. It was subtle at first. But it slowly grew brighter and brighter. Sophie, Hattie, and Owen watched in awe. It was the middle of the day, but Rory's light was dazzling.

"Your glow is so beautiful and bright," Sophie said.

But Rory shook his head. "I don't like seeing my light," he said quietly.

"Why not? You'd be like a star on stage," Hattie said.

Rory sighed. "That's just it," he explained. "When you're part of a troupe, you're not supposed to stand out. I wish my glow weren't so bright. Then I could blend in with the rest of the lightning bugs."

Sophie didn't quite understand. Who would ever want to dim their glow? Then again, Rory's life was so different from hers. The traveling.

The homeschooling. His tiny house and school on wheels.

Rory must know better than I do about what's best for the Lightning Bugs, she thought.

Chapter 6

It's Showtime!

At last, it was Friday. Sophie and her dad were headed out to the light show!

Sophie hurried to get her jacket. "Have a wonderful time," her mom said.

Winston was in a good mood, because he was going to make a dessert and play cards at home.

But he still reminded Sophie on her way out: "Remember everything for your painting!"

Outside, Sophie was surprised by how chilly it was after sunset. Mr. Mouse held up a lantern, and they made their way down the path.

Sophie looked around, taking in the forest at night. The full moon was bright and round in the starry sky. A cricket family chirped happily nearby.

Sophie looked to one side. Her dad's lantern cast a shadow onto the forest floor. Sophie giggled. Her shadow body was so long and stretched out! She wiggled her ears and arms and watched her shadow do the same.

Even in the dark, Sophie noticed
the show flyers they passed in the
forest. The flyers she had helped to
make! Sophie pointed them out to
her dad. They saw more and more
flyers as they kept getting closer to
Goldmoss Pond.

Soon Sophie and her dad caught up with Hattie. She was walking with her mom, dad, and big sister, Lydie.

Sophie and her dad walked the rest of the way with the Frog family. And who was right there at the show entrance, taking tickets?

"Rory!" Sophie shouted.

Rory smiled and waved. He took tickets from Mr. Mouse and Mrs. Frog. Then he handed them programs. "Enjoy the show!" Rory said.

Sophie wanted to stop and talk. But there were others behind them, waiting to get in. They had to move along.

"Where should we sit?" Hattie asked Sophie.

Sophie wasn't sure. This wasn't like Oak Hollow Theater, which had long log benches. Instead, the Lightning Bugs had placed rows of picnic blankets all around the pond.

"How about that one?" Mrs. Frog said.

She pointed at a large empty blanket by the water's edge. It was big enough for all six of them, with room to spare.

Once they settled down on the blanket, Sophie looked back at Rory. In the dark, his glow seemed even brighter. She could spot him so easily among the other lightning bugs.

Then Sophie squinted. A shadowy figure was taking a program from Rory. A familiar figure, now coming their way. Was it . . . ?

"Owen!" Hattie cried out.

It was Owen with his mom! He plopped down on their blanket. "I finally convinced my mom to bring me!" he said.

Mrs. Snake sat down next to him. "I'm still not sure about this," she said. "But Owen wanted to see the show so badly. And I kind of did too."

Sophie gazed up at the sky and smiled. It was hard to imagine this night getting any better. Now she *really* couldn't wait for the show to start!

— Chapter 7 —

All Eyes on the Sky

Across the pond, a quartet of lightning bugs began tuning their musical instruments.

"It's starting!" Owen said.

Audience members hurried to sit down. The murmur of excited chatter stopped, and the lights around the pond went dark. All eyes turned to the sky.

The quartet began to play. The notes lilted across the pond water.

Suddenly, an explosion of light lit
up the darkness!

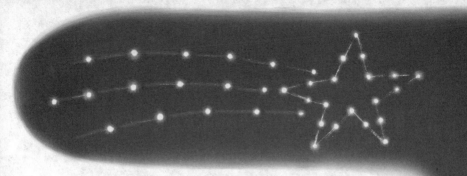

Sophie held her breath. Dozens of lightning bugs filled the air. At first, they looked like a random dusting of sparkles. But as Sophie watched, the points of light moved into formations.

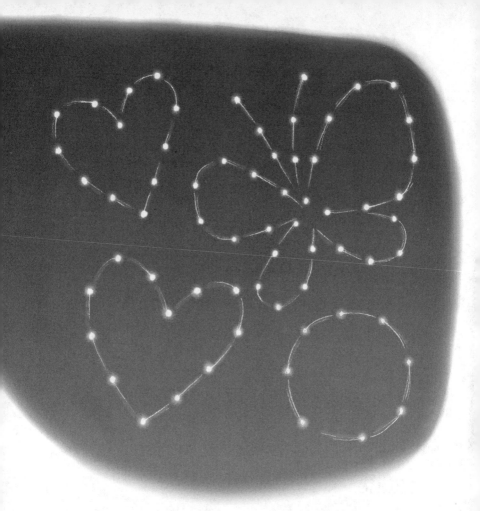

In time to the music, they created shapes. Circles! Stars! Hearts! Then a giant butterfly that flapped its wings!

"Amazing," Sophie whispered to Hattie.

Hattie pointed at the pond. "Look how the lights are reflected in the water. It's like a mirror!"

Hattie was right! Sophie tried hard to take a snapshot in her mind. She felt grateful that others were seeing the lights too. Maybe they could help her remember for Winston.

The show went on, with the lightning bugs creating different shapes. Then as the music got louder, the bugs spelled out a word: SILVERLAKE. Sophie gasped with delight.

The crowd cheered. And then the
sky went dark. Thunderous applause
echoed off the pond. Sophie clapped
and clapped until her hands tingled.

"Is it over?" she asked her dad as the lights in the audience turned back on.

George Mouse shook his head. "It's intermission," he explained. "There's still half to go."

What luck! thought Sophie.

They all lined up at a stand selling food and drinks. Sophie and her dad lined up first, then Hattie's family, and then Owen's family.

Sophie's dad bought her a cup of berry juice and an almond-coconut cookie. On the way back to the blanket, they talked about the first act.

"What do you think so far?" George Mouse asked her.

Sophie named her favorite parts. "The hearts!" she said. "And the SILVERLAKE, for sure!"

Then the Frog family returned to the blanket. "I loved the pinwheel," Hattie said.

"And the flower bouquet," added Lydie.

Then Mrs. Snake returned. "Has anyone seen Owen?" she asked, looking worried.

85

Sophie turned to look back toward the food and drink stand. "He was standing in line with us," she said.

Hattie nodded. "He was definitely behind me." But they hadn't seen him since.

"Owen!" Mrs. Snake called out.

They all raised their voices together as one: "One, two, three, O-WEN!"

There was no answer.

Mrs. Snake and the Frog family headed back toward the stand to look. Meanwhile, Mr. Mouse and Sophie started looking around in the audience.

Along the way, Sophie ran into Rory. "Have you seen Owen?" she asked him.

Rory looked confused. "No," he said. "Why? Is something wrong?"

"I don't know," Sophie said. "Owen is missing."

Chapter 8

Searching
the Shadows

Rory flew off to tell the rest of his troupe about Owen. And moments later, a lightning bug made an announcement to the crowd.

"Hello," she said through a megaphone. "Kindly look around you for a young snake named Owen. He seems to have gotten separated from his family and friends."

Sophie and her dad checked around all the blankets. Hattie and her mom looked around all the stands. The Lightning Bugs checked in and around the wagons.

But Owen was nowhere to be found at Goldmoss Pond.

They decided to widen the search. Mrs. Snake organized the searchers.

"I'll stay here and look again," she said. "Hattie, could you and your family check in the orchard? And maybe over by our house?"

The Frog family nodded and headed off.

"Sophie," Mrs. Snake continued, "can you and your dad check the schoolyard? Owen loves that playground."

Sophie led the way. In fact, she knew the way to school even better than her dad did.

But Sophie was glad to have him along—and his lantern. On the way to the show, the forest seemed so magical and exciting. Now everything felt different: colder, darker, and a little scary.

Looking for Owen reminded her of another scary time: the time she lost track of Winston near Butterfly Brook. Sophie's tummy did flips just remembering it. Looking for Owen felt similar . . . but worse, because it was so hard to see anything in the dark.

They arrived at the schoolyard. They looked all around. "Owen!" Sophie called out.

"Owen?" George Mouse called, checking up in the tree branches. "He's a good climber," he pointed out to Sophie.

That
reminded
Sophie. Owen
liked to climb up and
slide down Birch Tree
Slide. It wasn't far from the school.
"Let's go check there," she suggested.

So they headed on, calling Owen's
name the whole way.

As they neared Birch Tree Slide,
Sophie's ears twitched. "Shhh. Did
you hear that?" she asked her dad.

"Hear what?" George Mouse whispered.

A familiar voice called out from the other side of the slide. "O-wen?"

"Oh, it's Hattie!" Sophie said into the darkness.

Hattie and her family came out from behind the slide. "I guess we had the same idea," Lydie said.

Hattie started staring at the slide. "Do you see that?" Hattie asked. "Inside the slide. Something is . . . glowing."

Sophie looked. Sure enough, there was a light coming out of the bottom of the hollow branch. It grew brighter and brighter, until . . .

ZZZZZIP!

— Chapter 9 —

Rise
and Shine

A spark of light came rocketing out of the slide, landing in a pile of leaves.

"Whoa! What a ride!" Rory said. He picked himself up and dusted himself off. "I was looking for Owen in the tree branches. But then I tumbled into the slide." He laughed. "I can tell you for sure he's not inside there."

Hattie thanked Rory for helping with the search.

Rory shrugged. "Dad said to leave it to the grown-ups," he said. "But you all gave me the tour of Silverlake Forest. So I kind of know my way around."

Now they had plenty of light. Between Rory's super-bright glow and her dad's lantern, Sophie felt like they were walking around in broad daylight. Surely they could find Owen now!

They looked for him at Forget-Me-Not Lake. They searched around town, where all the shops were closed for the night.

But when they ended up back at Goldmoss Pond, they still hadn't found him. The Lightning Bugs had canceled the rest of the show. Everyone was looking for Owen.

Mrs. Snake hurried up to them. "Did you find him?" she asked. Then she looked at Rory. "My, your light is very bright!"

Just then, a bush next to Rory started rustling. They all looked at it. The bush was shaking!

Shake. Shake-shake. A couple of leaves fell to the ground. Branches parted.

A sleepy-looking snake slowly poked his head out.

They all gasped. It was Owen!

Owen squinted in the bright light. "What time is it?" he asked groggily.

His mom pulled him out the rest of the way. She wrapped him in a tight snake hug.

"Owen, I was so worried," Mrs. Snake told him. "What happened to you?"

Owen rubbed his eyes. "Well . . . it was intermission. I wandered down here to the water's edge. Then I saw this bush. It looked like the *perfect* hiding place for sneaky snake. So I wriggled in."

Owen yawned. It was another one of his huge snake yawns. "I guess I fell asleep. Until Rory's light woke me up."

"My light?" Rory echoed.

Owen rubbed his eyes again. "Yeah. Your light is so bright that I couldn't *not* wake up!"

Rory beamed. "I guess . . . I guess my bright light does come in handy sometimes," he said.

Mrs. Snake wasn't finished scolding her child. "I *knew* this show was too late for you," she said. "Owen, you cannot play sneaky snake. Especially at nighttime. Not without telling us!"

Owen frowned. "That wouldn't be very sneaky," he said. "But okay."

Chapter 10

The Encore

The very next evening, Sophie felt lucky to be back at Goldmoss Pond.

Since Friday's show was cut short, the Lightning Bugs were putting on a special make-up show. And the crowd was even bigger! Sophie and her mom were waiting in a long line to get in. This time, her dad had stayed home with Winston.

"I guess word got out about the show," Sophie said to Hattie. Hattie had also returned to see the make-up show.

Owen and his mom were back too. "No sneaky snake tonight," he promised.

A lightning bug took their tickets. Another handed them their programs.

Hmm, thought Sophie. *Where was Rory?*

The first act was stunning. They had brand-new formations. Spirals! Arrows! A yellow wagon with turning wheels! There was even new music to go along with it.

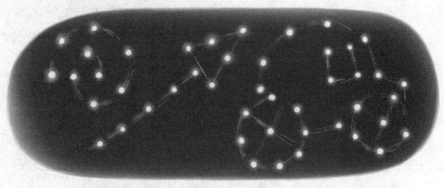

Sophie looked around for Rory during intermission. But she didn't see him then, either. *Maybe he's helping out behind the scenes tonight*, she thought.

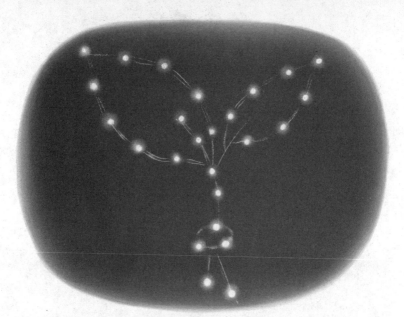

The second act began quietly. It told a story about a tree. A small seedling grew into a tree. Birds came to build nests in its branches. Fall came, and the leaves floated off the trees. After a long winter, spring came again, and the tree was surrounded by even more birds.

More and more lightning bugs
filled the sky over the pond. They gave
off such a glow that Sophie could see
the smiles on all the upturned faces.

A few lightning bugs flew over the audience. Everyone oohed and aahed.

Sophie noticed that one light was shining brighter than the others. Much brighter! And that lightning bug waved at her!

Sophie gasped. "There's Rory!" she cried out. She nudged Owen and Hattie. "Right there!"

They all waved
back at him. Then
they watched
in delight as he
finished the show as
the brightest one of all.

The crowd gave a standing
ovation. Then Sophie, Hattie, and
Owen rushed over to Rory's wagon
to congratulate him.

Rory thanked them all. "It felt
amazing to perform with my troupe!"
he told them. "I'm just sad we're
heading out of town tomorrow."

Sophie and her friends were sad too. "But I'm happy for the next town who gets to see your show," she told him. And she was happy for Rory and his life on the road.

Rory promised they'd be back again in a few summers.

Maybe by that time, Sophie thought, *Rory will be the star of the show! Winston will be old enough to attend the show, too.*

But until that day came, Sophie would do her best to capture the magical light show in the painting that she'd promised.

The End